Dial Books for Young Readers
Published by the Penguin Group
Penguin Group (USA) LLC
375 Hudson Street
New York, New York 10014

USA / Canada / UK / Ireland / Australia / New Zealand / India /
South Africa / China
penguin.com
A Penguin Random House Company
Copyright © 2014 by Rosie Winstead

Library of Congress Cataloging-in-Publication Data
Winstead, Rosie, author, illustrator.
Sprout helps out / by Rosie Winstead.   pages cm
  Summary: "Sprout loves to help her mom clean up around the
house and take care of her baby sister, but she sometimes makes a
bigger mess than she started with. Fortunately, Sprout has the best
intentions and is so sweet that even Mama doesn't mind"— Provided
by publisher.   ISBN 978-0-8037-3072-4 (hardcover)
[1. Helpfulness—Fiction.] I. Title.   PZ7.W7526Sp 2013
 [E]—dc23   2013008765

Manufactured in China on acid-free paper

10 9 8 7 6 5 4 3 2 1

Designed by Jennifer Kelly
Text set in Fontesque

Pencil, gouache, and watercolor paint were used when creating this book.

Sprout
Helps
Out

by
Rosie
Winstead

Dial Books for Young Readers
an imprint of Penguin Group (USA) LLC

Sprout is small.

But she is a BIG help.

And she knows it.

In the mornings, she makes the beds,

cooks,

and walks the fish—
he loves it!

Seasick

Then Sprout brushes ALL her teeth,
without even being reminded . . .

unlike others, who always forget.

After everyone is minty fresh,
Sprout puts MOM's toothbrush
back in its spot.

huuuuuuuh

mom's
Toothbrush

Sprout also does her own hair.

And it always looks perfect.

Tah-dah!

Now it's time to make
baby Bea laugh.

This is tricky for
most people.

But Sprout is . . .

OOPS!

. . . an expert.

After lunch, Bea wants to go outside.
So does everyone else.

Sprout takes them.

She is very good
at outside.

But OH NO!

Look at all this dirty laundry!

Now Sprout has to do the wash.

She's very good at it.

And she knows it.

Before

After

Ah, time for a break.

All done! Back to work!

Sprout fixes things
that are broken,

dusts,

and refreshes.

Ahhhchooo!

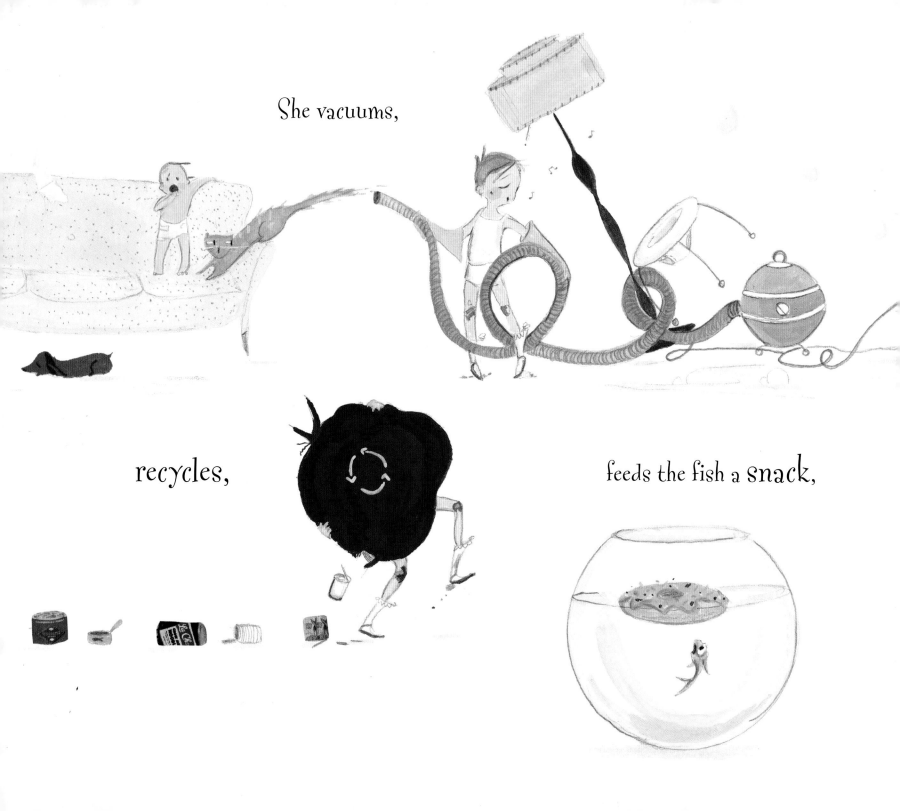

She vacuums,

recycles,

feeds the fish a snack,

does the dishes,

and puts things back . . .

POP!

where they belong.

Sprout's family is very lucky
to have her,

and they know it.